"Mother, don't make me take another basket of buns to Granny," pleaded Little Pink Riding Hood one morning. "She's so grumpy, and that silly wolf is always skulking around trying to frighten me."

But her mother wouldn't listen.

Granny is old and the wolf doesn't know any better. Just be polite and kind and everything will be alright.

Why should I?

thought Little Pink Riding Hood, crossly. "No one else is."

She hadn't gone very far when she met the wolf.

Hellooo,

he drooled.

But Little Pink wasn't in the mood.
"Oh, get lost!" she cried. "You need a
wash and your breath smells."

"Well, it can't be as dull as being nice all the time," said Little Pink Riding Hood. Then, she had a very naughty idea.

replied the wolf.

Little Pink settled down for a nap while the wolf bounded off. He hadn't gone far when he heard her snoring loudly.

he said.

At last, the wolf came to Granny's cottage. He went TAP-TAP on the door.

Who is it?

asked a gruff voice.

"It's your granddaughter," replied the wolf in a high-pitched voice.

The wolf shuffled inside and smiled sheepishly.
"Hello, Granny," he said, handing her the basket.

Not more buns,

said Granny, grumpily.

Then, she peered at the wolf.

Meanwhile, Little Pink Riding Hood woke up from her nap. "That was lovely," she said, stretching and yawning.

Then, she giggled.

No sooner had Little Pink spoken, than she heard the most alarming noises. There was a...

...CRASH,

BANG...

... and a terrible

HOWL!

"Oh, dear," she said, "I should go to Granny's house!"

Back at the cottage, Granny was chasing the wolf with an enormous axe.

I'm going to turn you into a handbag!

she roared, as she chased the terrified wolf round and round.

"Help!" howled the wolf, just as Little Pink Riding Hood opened the cottage door. "Something the matter?" she asked, innocently.

Your granny!

cried the wolf, diving to hide behind her.

Little Pink stepped aside and Granny lunged at the wolf with the axe. Seeing the sharp, glinting blade, he leapt out of the door and ran straight into Granny's bloomers, hanging on the washing line.

It's not every day that you see a wolf with pants on his head, bumping into trees,
said Little Pink Riding Hood, with a grin.
No, it isn't,
said Granny, and she laughed and laughed.

Little Pink Riding Hood thought that was a fantastic idea. She and Granny had loads of fun, and they became the best of friends.

As for the wolf, well, he was never seen again.